YAWWNNNNNN!

Love you!
Bye, Mama!

Have fun, Freddy!

MY TEACHER IS A
ROBOT
By Jeffrey Brown
Good morning, Fred.
CROWN BOOKS for YOUNG READERS New York

 Published in the United States by Crown Books for Young Readers, an imprint of Random House Children's Books, a division of Penguin Random House LLC, New York.

Crown and the colophon are registered trademarks of Penguin Random House LLC.

Visit us on the Web! rhcbooks.com

Educators and librarians, for a variety of teaching tools, visit us at RHTeachersLibrarians.com

Library of Congress Cataloging-in-Publication Data is available upon request.

ISBN 978-0-553-53451-1 (trade)
ISBN 978-0-553-53452-8 (lib. bdg.)
ISBN 978-0-553-53453-5 (ebook)

10 9 8 7 6 5 4 3 2 1

MANUFACTURED IN CHINA

First Edition

Random House Children's Books supports the First Amendment and celebrates the right to read.

Did you hear me, Fred? How are we starting the day?
Alejandra
Miriam
Derek
Edgar
Latasha

TEST?! I knew it! Another test so you can assign numbers to all of us for when you become our ROBOT OVERLORD!

What? No, I was saying I'm going to test your writing skills.
I bet we aren't even allowed to use our imaginations!
Of course you can!

Really?
Yes! It's CREATIVE writing!
You can write whatever you want!